I Don't Want To Go To Hospital

Tony Ross

Andersen Press
London

To Beth,
who liked hospital

Copyright © 2000 by Tony Ross
The rights of Tony Ross to be identified as the author and illustrator of this work
have been asserted by him in accordance with the Copyright, Designs and Patents Act, 1988.
First published in Great Britain in 2000 by Andersen Press Ltd., 20 Vauxhall Bridge Road,
London SW1V 2SA. Published in Australia by Random House Australia Pty.,
20 Alfred Street, Milsons Point, Sydney, NSW 2061. All rights reserved.
Colour separated in Switzerland by Photolitho AG, Zürich.
Printed and bound in Italy by Grafiche AZ, Verona.

10   9   8   7   6   5   4   3   2

British Library Cataloguing in Publication Data available.

ISBN 0 86264 968 4

This book has been printed on acid-free paper

"Ooo, Oww, Ooo," cried the Little Princess.
"My nose hurts!"

"You've got a little lump up there," said the Doctor.

"I'll get it out," said the General, drawing his sword.

"No," said the Doctor, "it won't come out. Her Majesty must go to hospital."

"No!" cried the Princess. "I don't want to go to hospital!"

"It's nice in hospital," said the Doctor. "You'll get sweets and cards."

"I don't want to go," said the Princess.

"It's nice in hospital," said the Queen, who had been there.

"I don't want to go," said the Princess.

"You'll meet lots of new friends in hospital,"
said the Prime Minister.

"No! I don't *want* to go to hospital," said the Princess, and she ran out of the room.

"Where is the Princess?" cried the Queen.
"It's time to go."

"She's not in her room," said the Maid.

"She's not in the dustbin," said the Cook.

"She's not in any of my boats," said the Admiral.

"She's not on the roof," said the Gardener.

"She's in the attic!" said the King.
"I don't want to go to hospital," said the Princess.

But the Little Princess had to go.

And the lump came out of her nose.

"Now you are better," said the Queen, "you can brush your teeth, and comb your hair . . .

. . . and tidy your room, and . . . "
"No!" cried the Princess . . .

". . . I want my tonsils out!"

"But why?" said the Queen.
"I want to go back to hospital," said the Little Princess.

"They treated me like a Princess in there."

Other *Little Princess* Picture Books

I Want My Potty
I Want To Be
I Want My Dinner
I Want A Sister

Little Princess Board Books

Shapes, Weather, Pets, Bedtime
I Want My Potty